Diogo

Out of this World

TEAM SONG

by Sally Odgers

illustrated by Matt Lin

S P A C E S P O R T S

First published in 2007
by Macmillan Education Aus

Copyright © 2007 Laguna Ba
www.lagunabaypublishing.co

Text by Sally Odgers
Illustrations by Matt Lin
Cover Design Allison Parry
Design by Matt Lin/Goblin D
Managing Editor Nicola Robinson

Out of this World: Team Song
ISBN 978 1407 10182 8

Printed by Tien Wah Press, Singapore

1 2 3 4 5 6 7 8 9   9 0 1 2 3 4 5 6 7 8

SPACE SPORTS

Contents

1   Globes and Anchors   5

2   On the Holoscreen   13

3   Jaff Interrupts   21

4   The Plan   31

5   Audition in Klikwitz Square   37

6   I Agree   48

7   Team Song   56

    Nova Speak   63

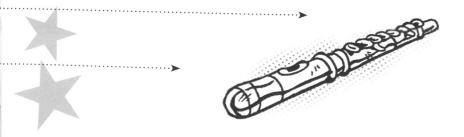

Three kinds of people live on Space Station Nova.

The Stationborn have been there for generations.

The Prof

Luke

Jaff

Janna

The Shipborn were born on giant spaceships that wander the Galaxy.

Pavros

The Earthborn came to Nova from Earth.

Ellie

There has always been rivalry between the three sets of Stationers but one thing brings them together: the game they call 3D.

chapter 1

Globes and Anchors

Sometimes space station life was just too busy. You had to choose what was most important – and what you'd miss out. And that, sighed Janna, was a big hassle.

She had to do schoolwork. She had regular 3D practices with Gold Team Junior. She had to help her stepmother, Hindel, with the Space Station *Nova*'s green-ox system. Then there was music. For years she had sung while her brother Jaff played his flute.

The twins had been born on the wandering starship *Troubadour*. The captain, Minstrel, made sure everyone learned to sing and play. Janna and

Jaff were his prize pupils. For the twins, making music was as natural as breathing. It was what they did best.

Except, Janna decided, for 3D. Now they lived on *Nova*, 3D practice took more time than Janna could spare – but she loved it. She didn't love singing any less, but music would always be there. In a couple more years she'd be too old for Gold Team Junior. There were senior 3D teams but nobody cared much about them. The juniors were the stars.

Helping Hindel was important – she guessed. And 3D was very important.

Yes, music could wait. When she was grown up, she and Jaff could leave *Nova* and rove the galaxy as star-gypsies, playing and singing on starships, planets and stations, just as they'd always planned.

Janna was frowning as she headed down the spiral walkway to the 3D dome. Jaff had been so angry when she'd told him Coach Meriwether had called a special practice.

"You promised we could rehearse 'Galaxy Crazy' today!"

"We can rehearse any time. The team can only practise when Coach Meriwether books the dome."

"What if a star-gypsy agent comes? We'd look like space-brains if we mess up our act."

"Jaff, we have *years* to rehearse. We can do it in our sleep."

"An agent might come next week," argued Jaff.

"Or in five years' time." Or never, Janna thought.

"Or tomorrow. Remember what Captain said – he'd send someone to check our progress."

Janna chewed her lip. Captain Minstrel might send an agent to *Nova* one day, but not without warning. And it wouldn't be soon. The *Troubadour* was light years away…

"Let me know when it happens," she snapped. "And you might as well know: I have another practice at 0700 tomorrow." She walked out.

It wasn't *her* fault Jaff was lonely. It wasn't *her* fault their father had uprooted his children from the *Troubadour* to settle on Space Station *Nova*. They'd been here for two years now, so why couldn't Jaff accept it? The people of *Nova* were not musical. They had other interests. Why couldn't Jaff find something else he loved to do, as she had done? Music would still be there when they were older.

"Janna! Hey!"

Janna saw her friend Ellie waving from E-level. A single globe earring bobbed and glittered in the light as Ellie turned her head.

"You got your ear globe then!" Janna tried not to sound envious as Ellie hurried up to the walkway. "Did it hurt?"

Ellie grinned, and touched the earring with a careful forefinger. "You should have heard Pav squeal when they put *his* in."

Pavros was Ellie's elder brother, and the captain of Gold Team Junior. He was tall, dark, handsome and superior. Janna couldn't imagine him squealing.

She watched the ear globe twinkle. It was so typical of Mayor Klikwitz to decide the Earthborn should have something so special. Just because *he* was Earthborn.

Ellie caught her eye and grinned. Then she sniffed and tilted her nose in the air. "We Earthborn," she announced, mimicking Mayor Klikwitz's smug voice, "are the natural leaders of this station. We must show pride in our heritage." She dropped back into her normal manner. "That's why *we* have globes while you Shipborn have little anchor tatts. As for those Birth Marks the Stationborn have... eyewww!"

Janna laughed, and touched the earring gently, making it spin. The coloured shapes that marked the continents and oceans of Earth glittered.

"Ow," said Ellie. "We'd better go. If one of us is late Coach Meriwether might throw us off the team." She sounded half serious because on *Nova* 3D was a very serious business.

"Race you, then!" Janna took off down the walkway. She beat Ellie, just, to the 3D dome, and turned to beam at her in triumph. Ellie had her hand over her ear and grinned back. "Ouch!"

Brig Meriwether cleared his throat. "You're late."

"Sorry, Coach," said Ellie, noticing Luke and Pav had already arrived. "I just—"

"I can see you have your ear globe, Ellie. Congratulations." The coach winked at Janna. "Makes our anchors look small."

"That's what I was thinking," said Janna. The tiny silver tattoo that designated her as Shipborn had been on the back of her hand ever since she could remember. Brig Meriwether had one too.

"Enough!" said Meriwether. "I called this special practice for a reason. Gold Team Junior will be playing in the finals of the interstellar championships!"

The announcement swept earrings, tattoos and Jaff out of Janna's mind. Along with the other three, she punched the air and cheered. Luke, the newest member of Gold Team Junior, turned a cartwheel.

Coach Meriwether held up his hand. "I'm sure you all know what this means, team."

"It means we're the *best*!" yelled Luke.

"*One* of the best," said Meriwether. "If we want to make sure we are *the* best, we need to get more practice. Starting today, it's double time in the dome."

Pav, Ellie and Luke whooped with delight. Janna chewed her lip. Double time in the dome? She might as well give up her music completely.

chapter 2

On the Holoscreen

When they had lived on the *Troubadour*, Jaff's flute playing and Janna's singing had made them special. Then, on the voyage from Sirius to Vega3, Dad had met Hindel, and now they were all living on Space Station *Nova*.

Straight away, Hindel had urged Jaff and Janna to try out for the junior 3D team.

"You'll love it!" she insisted. "It's great exercise. I used to play Gold Attack position when I was your age."

To please Hindel, the twins tried out. Jaff failed to get past the first round. Janna beat hundreds of other kids to become the team's Gold Saver.

She had promised Jaff that nothing would change but it had, of course.

And here was Janna rushing off to yet another practice.

Jaff pulled his flute from the pocket of his ship-suit and left the unit. If Hindel heard him playing, she'd want him to help with the green-ox system in the ecology level. He could just hear her now. "Jaff, you know the human body needs exercise to keep healthy. You know *Nova* needs a balance of plants and filters to keep the air fresh. We must never neglect our health *or* the station's."

Captain Minstrel used to say Jaff should never neglect his music. Who was right, Hindel or Captain Minstrel? When a star-gypsy agent signed him and Janna up, *everyone* would see.

Jaff slipped down the spiral walkway towards Klikwitz Square, passing public holoscreens on the way. News bites flickered in a never-ending parade.

EARTHBORN WEAR EAR GLOBES WITH PRIDE, MAYOR KLIKWITZ STATES. ✪ GRISSOM BROTHERS EXPELLED FROM NOVA FOR USING BLANKOUT TO MAKE THEMSELVES INVISIBLE. KLIKWITZ TELLS THEM: "DON'T COME BACK!" ✪ KLIKWITZ'S POPULARITY

INVISIBLE. KLIKWITZ TELLS THEM: 'DON'T COME BACK!' ✪ KLIKWITZ'S POPU

Jaff shook his head. The Grissom brothers gave the Shipborn a bad reputation.

✪ KLIKWITZ'S POPULARITY AT ALL-TIME HIGH. ✪ KLIKWITZ'S

Huh! Who said so? Klikwitz?

GOLD TEAM JUNIOR TO COMPETE IN INTERSTELLAR CHAMPIONSHIP

FINALS. ✪ GARBAGE RECYCLING DATES TO CHANGE FROM THU

Gold Team Junior had made the finals? Jaff tried to be glad for Janna's sake but it was impossible.

"3D," he muttered. "Mayor Klikwitz. Doesn't anyone on this stupid station ever think of anything important?"

His beeper chimed. Jaff snorted. It was probably Janna apologising for being so selfish. Or it might be Hindel.

His thumb hovered over the "reject" button. He needn't answer Janna but he'd be in trouble if he ignored Hindel.

Reluctantly, Jaff thumbed "read".

Greetings, JAFF TROUBADOUR: Your entry in the Interstellar Star-Gypsy Contest is a semi-finalist. To claim your prize, click "I AGREE TO ABIDE BY CONTEST RULES' now.

Jaff had seen the Interstellar Star-Gypsy Contest advertised on a holoscreen weeks ago. There was no entry fee and it promised lots of prizes. Jaff had entered a holo of Janna and himself performing 'Galaxy Crazy' during their last days on the *Troubadour*.

This wasn't the first musical contest he'd entered but he'd never heard back from any of them before. He hadn't even told Janna.

They were through to the semi-finals? His hand trembled as he clicked on "I AGREE" and waited breathlessly to see his prize. It might be a new flute, or a five-cred voucher for a new music chip. Or a signed holo of a famous star-gypsy. Or – or –

The beeper chimed again.

Your prize is a free audition with star-gypsy agent Tarza Rhymer. Click "I AGREE" to accept this opportunity.

An audition with a star-gypsy agent! That was the best prize ever… but hey, why was he surprised? Captain Troubadour had always said he and Janna were going to be stars. Jaff felt a big smile curving his mouth. An audition! Wait until Janna heard this!

The beeper chimed a third time, and Jaff's thumb stabbed down hard. This time, the incoming message was an audio-visual-byte. He stared, fascinated, at the face that appeared on his beeper screen.

"Jaff Troubadour?"

"Y-yes!" Jaff gulped.

"My name is Tarza Rhymer," said the caller. "Congratulations on your wonderful entry in our Interstellar Star-Gypsy Contest."

"Thank you! Janna and I—"

"Your free audition is scheduled for 0700 tomorrow," continued Tarza Rhymer.

0700. Janna had a practice then.

Jaff frowned. "That time is a bit difficult."

"Would you rather not audition? There is a cancellation fee of fifty credits."

"The audition is meant to be free!" blurted Jaff.

"The audition is free if you take it but there are costs involved for the agency."

"Could we make it another time? Earlier?" begged Jaff. "Or another day?"

Rhymer looked shocked. "Is that what you'd say to a starship captain who wanted to hire you? Star-gypsies need dedication and commitment. Since you don't have these, the chance must go to the next best entry..."

"We'll be there," said Jaff. Janna would just have to be late for practice, for once. She owed him that much.

"Wise decision. I'll see you at Klikwitz Square at 0700 tomorrow." Tarza Rhymer smiled.

"What happens if we pass?" asked Jaff.

"Then you go into the finals. You will also sign up with the Tarza Rhymer agency, and we'll talk about tours." She vanished.

Star-gypsies travelled the galaxy. Star-gypsies could name their price, live where they chose, and do what they wanted. They were welcome on every inhabited planet, and could travel free on every starship. They were even more famous than 3D players because their careers lasted so much longer.

A star-gypsy had money and respect. A star-gypsy might leave Space Station *Nova* and never come back.

Jaff began to run. He was heading for the 3D dome on the recreation level.

chapter 3
Jaff Interrupts

Jaff shouldered through the crowd at the 3D dome. The coach, Brig Meriwether, was directing the practice.

Stop. Start. Toss. Dive.

Janna was playing Gold Saver position. As Jaff stared, willing her to look his way, she leapt in a spectacular sequence she called a "deflect-and-roll". She somersaulted to land lightly on her feet, a red ball clutched in her left hand.

Jaff heard the crowd gasp. These stationers thought that was clever, did they? Had they ever heard Janna sing the gentle "Ship Song"? Had they heard her sing the wild "Galaxy Crazy" song?

How could they think throwing stupid balls into stupid slots in a stupid 3D dome was more important than that?

Janna smashed the final red ball out of its slot and Pavros flicked a gold one into its place.

"Gold high score!" called Coach Meriwether and he cut the gravity.

The red holoteam vanished. Janna felt a wide smile break out. Pav had scored the final goal but *she* had made room for the shot. That was teamwork at its best.

She caught Luke's heel as he passed her, flipping him into a roll. She was still laughing as Gold Team Junior left the dome.

"Not bad," said Coach Meriwether.

"Not bad!" Ellie snorted. "We were brilliant!"

"You need to work on your – yes?" The coach's sentence broke off as someone shouldered through the crowd. "Is anything wrong?"

Janna stared at her brother. Jaff *never* came to 3D practices.

"I have to speak to Janna." Jaff looked pale and distracted.

"I'm giving the team notes," said Meriwether pleasantly. "Janna won't be long."

"I need to speak to her *now*."

Coach Meriwether nodded to Janna. "Go ahead, but be quick."

"Well?" said Janna. Jaff grabbed her arm and pulled her aside, his hand shaking with excitement.

"Janna... there's a star-gypsy agent coming to audition us."

"A–" Janna frowned at her brother. "Oh, Jaff... not that *again!*"

"Really! If we pass, we go into the finals in the Interstellar Star-Gypsy Contest!"

"The what?"

"I entered a holo of us doing 'Galaxy Crazy'. This agent, Tarza Rhymer, is coming here to audition us for a contract and a star-gypsy tour. In the morning." Jaff was speaking so fast his words fell over one another.

Janna felt a surge of excitement. Star-gypsying

had always been their ambition, but she couldn't believe the chance had come already. "But we're too young. Don't you have to be sixteen?"

"She didn't say that."

"Things like that don't just happen. The odds are thousands to one."

"Really?" demanded Jaff. "What were the odds of you making the 3D team?"

"That's different."

"Yes, this is much more important!" Jaff shook her arm. "This is our big chance, Janna. We can get off this station and back where we belong."

"But—"

Jaff grinned at her. "Tell your coach to find a new player. The star-gypsy twins are out of here!"

"Janna?" Coach Meriwether was staring across at them. "Have you finished? Is everything all right?"

"Everything is wonderful," said Jaff.

"Then let your sister get back to work," said Meriwether.

Janna walked back to the coach. Her feet felt far away, as if someone had cut the gravity again.

If she and Jaff passed the audition, everything would change. If they failed, everything would stay as it was.

Should she warn Brig Meriwether he might need to train a new player for the interstellar 3D finals? What if he thought she had lost interest in 3D? He might put her off the team immediately. There was always a long queue of hopeful players waiting for a vacancy. Then, if she and Jaff failed the audition, she'd have given up 3D for nothing.

As she left the recreation level, Jaff joined her. He was still fizzing with excitement.

"Slow down," said Janna at last. "Jaff, focus! Tell me *exactly* what's going on."

Jaff drew a deep breath. "I entered the holo of us performing 'Galaxy Crazy' in the Interstellar Star-Gypsy contest."

"I've never heard of that before."

"It's new, I suppose."

"Who's running it? One of the starship captains?"

Jaff flipped his hand vaguely, and said he didn't know. "It was advertised on the holoscreens. I beeped for more information and sent the holo in. You know, the one we did on our farewell from the *Troubadour*?"

"You entered the contest without telling me?"

"We could have made a new holo and entered together but you were too busy. Remember? Anyway, I entered. Then today the agent, Tarza Rhymer, beeped me to say we've won a free audition. If we pass, we sign with an agency and go into the finals. We go on a star-gypsy tour."

"What agency? How can we tour at our age?"

"I suppose they've changed the rules since we left *Troubadour*." Jaff scowled at her. "We can ask at the audition."

"Where do we have to go for that?"

"Klikwitz Square, tomorrow at 0700."

"Tomorrow at 0700!" said Janna, staring. "We can't do that, Jaff. I have a practice then. Besides, we haven't rehearsed!"

"And whose fault is that? Haven't I begged and begged

you to rehearse with me? But no – all you cared about was 3D."

Jaff's voice had become shrill, and Janna looked at him in dismay.

"3D is important to me," she said.

"And music isn't?"

They were still glaring at one another when Ellie caught up and draped an arm around each twin. "What are you two fighting about?"

Jaff pulled away from Ellie. "We've won the chance to audition for a star-gypsy agent!" he snapped. "Janna's being stupid."

Ellie stared from one to the other. "What's a star-gypsy agent? What are you talking about?"

chapter 4

The Plan

"**D**on't you Earthborn know *anything?*" snarled Jaff.

"Tell me now," said Ellie.

Janna opened her mouth to explain but Jaff got in first. As they walked towards E-level with Ellie, Jaff told the Earthborn girl all about their ambitions. He told how Captain Minstrel had trained them and how they'd vowed to keep up their rehearsals while they were living on *Nova*.

When he had finished, Ellie clapped her hands. "Why didn't you ever tell me you could sing, Janna?"

Janna looked down at her toes. "I didn't think you'd be interested."

"You must be *really* good to get to the semis in an interstellar music contest!" Ellie exclaimed. "If it was me, I'd be telling the galaxy!"

"But the audition is at 0700 tomorrow," Janna protested. "And we have a 3D practice then. I *can't* miss a practice."

"Of course you can't miss a practice," said Pavros who had caught up with them. "Why would you?"

Janna groaned. It was bad enough that Jaff had been telling Ellie their business, but Pav was the captain of the 3D team. She willed the others to drop the subject but Jaff said, "Janna and I entered an interstellar contest. We have an audition with a star-gypsy agent at 0700 tomorrow at Klikwitz Square."

"What, singing and stuff? La-la-la? Is that all?"

"What do you mean: *all*?" yelled Jaff. "You guys don't care about anything but 3D!"

Pavros looked superior. "This is an interstellar final we're practising for," he said coldly.

"Yes... and this is our *future*," said Jaff. "Music is more important than any stupid game."

"Janna doesn't think so," retorted Pavros.

"You Earthborn never think anyone else has rights."

"And you Shipborn want to have it all." Pavros grinned suddenly. "*You* go to this audition since it's so important to you. Janna can come to the practice. There. Problem solved."

Jaff sighed. "The audition is for both of us. We work as a team."

Pavros raised one eyebrow. "Huh?"

"I play the flute. Janna sings. Half an act is no better than half a 3D team."

There was a silence.

"What happens if you pass this audition?" said Pavros.

"We go into the finals. The agent will sign us up and we'll go on a star-gypsy tour."

Pav pulled out his beeper. "I'm going to find out more about this contest."

"What's to find out?" said Jaff. "It's a contest! It was on the holoscreens. The audition is tomorrow!"

"Just wait here." Pav strolled away, keying on his beeper as he went.

"What's he doing?" yelled Jaff. "This is nothing to do with him!"

Ellie and Janna stared at him. They were used to Pavros taking charge of things.

After a few minutes, Pavros returned. "Janna can do the audition," he announced.

"But I'll be late for practice!"

"We will *all* be late for practice," said Pavros grandly. "We'll come and watch. Coach won't throw us *all* off the team. Ellie, let Luke know what's going on."

While Janna was still staring at Pav, Luke's face appeared on the screen of Ellie's beeper.

"Why don't we just ask Coach to change the practice?" he suggested.

"He might also say Janna has to choose music *or* 3D," said Ellie. "If she passes the audition, we can tell him then."

Luke agreed doubtfully, and just like that the plan was made.

✪ ✪ ✪

Having her teammates' support should have made Janna feel better but she went to bed that night with a bad feeling. Why had Pavros suggested a plan that would get him into trouble? He was the team leader. Why was he doing this? She had a nasty feeling she knew.

She sat up and beeped Pavros.

"What?" he asked, sleepily.

"You expect us to fail this audition, don't you?"

"How would I know?" Pav yawned. "I've never heard you sing. I expect you'll pass, though."

"Why are you helping us then? You can't want me off the team?"

"You won't be off the team, Janna," said Pavros confidently.

"I can't be on the team if I'm touring."

Visibly, Pav changed his mind about keeping her in suspense. "Star-gypsies have to be at least sixteen to tour," he said. "I checked the rules with – I mean, I researched it. Even if you win this contest outright you'll be too old to play for Gold Team Junior long before you're sixteen."

"Oh," said Janna. Jaff had been so sure their ages didn't matter but if Pav had checked...

Pavros yawned again. "See you in the morning, Jan. And just *don't* sign anything until someone older has checked it for you."

He disappeared from her beeper screen.

chapter 5

Audition in Klikwitz Square

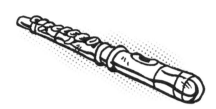

Janna didn't tell Jaff what Pavros had said. Let the agent explain that they were too young to tour, even if they made the finals. The audition wouldn't be wasted. The agent would note their names and, when they *were* old enough, they could start straight away. It was going to be all right. She really *could* have her music *and* 3D.

As she prepared for the audition, Janna daydreamed. She saw herself and Jaff, at sixteen, leaving *Nova* on a starship. Perhaps it would be the *Troubadour*.

The costume she'd worn on the *Troubadour* wouldn't fit. The silver anchor that decorated the front was stretched out of shape.

Jaff couldn't fit into his costume either. "We'll have new ones soon," he said. "Proper star-gypsy outfits." He sounded happy and confident, and Janna winced. She was getting exactly what she wanted, but Jaff was going to be disappointed.

"Where are you two off to so early?" asked Hindel.

"I have a 3D practice, remember?" said Janna. She couldn't face any more explanations. "We'll tell her the truth later," she excused herself as Jaff hustled her down to the first walkway.

"Exactly." Jaff nodded. "It's better to give people a *fait accompli*."

"A what?"

"*Fait accompli*," repeated Jaff. "It means, something that's already been decided or done." He paused, then added, "Like when you told me you'd joined the 3D team."

"What do you mean by that? You tried out for it too."

"Only to stop Hindel nagging!" snapped Jaff.

"But… you saw me go through all the rounds. So how could it be a *fait… fait…*"

"*Accompli*," said Jaff. "I knew Coach Meriwether was going to offer you a place on the team. I didn't think you'd be mean enough to take it."

"You should have said you didn't want me to."

If Jaff *had* said so would she have given up the chance to play 3D with Gold Team Junior?

Janna honestly didn't know. She tried to turn it around in her head. What if Jaff was chosen to be a star-gypsy and she wasn't? How bad would she feel? Would she expect him to give up his chance?

Nonsense. Jaff hadn't *wanted* to play 3D.

Janna shook off the uncomfortable thoughts. Nothing could happen for years yet. Pav had said so.

✪ ✪ ✪

Klikwitz Square was a small dome with its own green-ox system. A sound stage reared to one side. Mayor Klikwitz used it when he made his speeches.

Right in the middle of the square stood a giant statue of the mayor, with a viewing platform built into the head. Jaff had often wanted to climb it but today he was looking for the agent. "It's 0700," he said. "She should be here."

On cue, Tarza Rhymer appeared from the gravity-chute behind the statue. The star-gypsy agent was wearing high boots and a sharp-tailed dress with points that hung stiffly by her ankles. "Jaff Troubadour?" she asked, coming swiftly forward. She took out a noter. "I have a contract for you to sign, Jaff."

"Doesn't the audition come first?" asked Jaff.

The agent laughed. "That's just a formality. I can tell you your entry was one of the most impressive I've ever seen. The piece you did is one of my favourites."

"'Galaxy Crazy'?" said Jaff.

"That's right. 'Galaxy Crazy'. I love that tune." She glanced at Janna. "Have you come to watch, or are you a singer too?"

"She *is* the singer from the holo," reminded Jaff. "I play the flute. She sings." He felt his heart beating uncomfortably. "Has there been a mistake?"

Tarza Rhymer glanced at her noter and touched a key. She frowned. "Oh, I see what's happened. My assistant must have mixed up the notes. Of course... you two perform together. I was thinking of another boy who sang 'Galaxy Crazy' as well."

Jaff felt his panic subsiding. Anyone could make a mistake. He reached for the noter.

Janna trod on Jaff's toe. "Would you excuse us just a minute?" she said to Tarza Rhymer. "We need to discuss something."

Jaff protested as she dragged him away to the other end of the sound stage. "What are you doing? She's going to sign us up!"

"We mustn't sign anything yet," said Janna. "We need to get someone older to check it for us. Pav said—"

"Pav!" Jaff felt anger bubbling inside him. "Pav, Pav, Pav! What does he know? He's just trying to stop you from passing the audition."

"He doesn't care if I pass or not. He checked the rules. Nothing has changed. You still have to be sixteen to tour."

"How did we get into the semi-finals?" spat Jaff. "We were *ten* when we made that holo."

Janna shrugged. "I don't know but I'm sure Pav's right." She nodded in Tarza's direction. "Ask her to show you the rules if you don't want to take Pav's word for it."

"I will then! You'll see. She said we'd talk about tours."

"And one more thing," said Janna softly. "I don't think she even watched the holo you sent."

"Of course she did!"

"Come on, Jaff! Use your brain. She raved over it but she didn't even know there were two of us!"

"She explained all that. Her assistant mixed up the notes."

"But she said 'Galaxy Crazy' was one of her favourite pieces. *And* that a single singer also did it. Remember? It's not the kind of song you mix up with anything else and it *has* to have two performers. If you sing it without music there are big gaps in the tune."

"Maybe she knows a different version."

Janna held out her hand. "I have an idea. Let's say we're going to perform 'Galaxy Crazy' for her, but do something different. 'Ship Song', maybe? If she corrects us, then she really does know what she's talking about. If not..."

"That's so stupid! You'll ruin our chances! We've *got* to do the right song."

"Have you quite finished your discussion?" asked Tarza Rhymer coolly.

"Yes!" said Jaff. "Janna—"

"Since 'Galaxy Crazy' is one of your favourites, we could do that," Janna said quickly.

"I'd love to hear it again," said Rhymer. "But do hurry. I have other acts to see."

Jaff blew a soft note on the flute. Janna began to hum gently, her voice moving in waves.

Jaff almost choked. Janna was doing just what she had suggested. This wasn't the opening to "Galaxy Crazy" at all! She was beginning "Ship Song"! He had two choices: he could go along with Janna and wait for the agent to interrupt, or he could stop playing right now.

But Captain Minstrel said you must *always* go on once you'd started a performance. Jaff took a deeper breath and let the flute follow Janna's humming.

A flash of movement at the top of the mayor's statue caught his eye and he almost lost his place in the tune. He *must* concentrate.

Surely any star-gypsy agent must know "Ship Song", the anthem of the Shipborn? It was nothing like the piece he had entered in the contest.

Then Janna began to sing.

> *Ship of the galaxy, stars of the sea,*
> *Whispering waves in the silence of space...*
> *Song of the keel with the currents of time*
> *Satellites swinging, celestial grace...*
> *Stars of the sea in the silence of space*
> *Currents of time in celestial grace.*

Janna's voice faded back into a hum as Jaff took up a counter melody. Tarza Rhymer was busily keying information into her noter. Was she listening to them? Or was she noting that the Troubadour Twins couldn't tell one tune from another? He let the flute sob as he saw their chances slipping away. This was all Janna's fault!

His sister gave the tiny nod to show she was moving into the last refrain.

Ship of the galaxy, luminously
Sailing for ever, the Shipborn at sea.

Jaff played the last plaintive phrases and then lowered his flute. He held his breath.

Tarza Rhymer beamed. "That was perfect. Even better than the holo." She held the noter out. "Now... I need you both to sign right here."

I Agree

Jaff longed to sign the noter but Janna was right. There *was* something wrong.

Either Tarza Rhymer had a very bad memory or she was telling lies. Neither was the kind of thing Jaff expected from a reputable agent.

Janna reached for the noter and began to read aloud from the info screen.

"Just sign," urged the agent. "Right there."

"I agree to attend the recommended training classes..." read Janna aloud. She looked up. "What classes?"

Rhymer waved one hand and pushed the other through her spiky hair. "These classes are to bring out the best of your talent," she said.

That sounds all right, thought Jaff. Every musician needs to learn, and he and Janna were out of practice.

Janna read on. "I agree that costume purchase, holo-advertising fees, training fees and retainers will be my responsibility." She looked directly at Jaff. "There seem to be a lot of fees in this, considering it's a prize."

"The *audition* was the prize," Jaff pointed out. "And we paid for our costumes on *Troubadour*, didn't we?"

"This is different. We're supposed to agree to pay for something without knowing the price?"

The agent smiled. "What a very suspicious person you are, Janna. You don't have to pay for costumes or classes if you don't want to! Or for advertising."

"That's all right then," said Jaff. Wasn't it?

"Of course..." added Rhymer, "you would be foolish not to. I suppose the bottom line is this: do you want to be successful star-gypsies or just nobodies from a space station?"

Ouch! thought Jaff. Janna wasn't a nobody; she was the Gold Saver of Gold Team Junior. Everyone on *Nova* knew Janna Troubadour was special. But what was he? Janna's twin brother, who didn't play 3D.

"Captain Minstrel said we should never give up our music!" he said. "He said we should take every chance that came our way with both hands. Maybe this is what he meant."

"Exactly," said Tarza Rhymer.

"If we need all those things to succeed, we'd better forget it for now," said Janna. "We can't pay for them."

Rhymer smiled. "Oh, so that's the problem! You wouldn't be asked to pay for anything *now*. It would come out of your earnings when you start touring."

"But that's years away," said Janna. "By then we could owe millions of credits."

The agent was still smiling but her eyes looked angry. She sighed, loudly. "It's obvious *you* don't want this chance, Janna, but you have no right to deprive your brother. Jaff can sign up alone. He's the one with the real talent in any case."

Jaff wanted to believe her. He had hardly admitted it to himself but he had felt resentful ever since Janna had joined Gold Team Junior.

He didn't want to play 3D but hearing people cheering for his twin made him feel invisible. Janna spent more time with Pav, Ellie and Luke than she did with him. She neglected her music, leaving him no one to rehearse with.

Surely it was only fair that *he* should get his chance now? But did the agent know what she was talking about?

"That audition we just did," he said slowly. "You said it was perfect. Better than the holo I entered."

Rhymer shrugged.

"You have real star quality, but your sister's singing was nothing special."

So. Now he knew the truth about Tarza Rhymer. She was a liar.

"You don't know what you're talking about," he said. "Everyone knows Janna's singing is very special. Everyone who understands music, I mean." He sighed, seeing his hopes vanish. "I won't sign up with you either." He forced a smile. "So, thanks for the audition. We'll go now. Janna has a 3D practice."

"Fine!" said Rhymer. She snatched the noter from Janna and began to key in information.

"You can go then… as soon as you pay what you owe me." She stabbed viciously at the keys.

"We don't owe anything!" snapped Jaff. "This was a free audition."

"You owe me for two breached agreements, plus travel, plus inconvenience, plus—"

"We never agreed to anything!" cried Janna.

"Your brother did." Tarza Rhymer snapped up another screen and waved it in front of Janna. "See? I AGREE, twice over. That *is* your brother's sig-key, is it not?"

Janna turned to Jaff. "What have you done?"

"I only agreed to abide by the contest rules!" cried Jaff.

"Which you obviously didn't read." Another screen sprang open, and Rhymer read aloud: "All costs associated with claiming prizes shall be paid by the winners. All payments must be made in full. All agreements are binding. All—"

The agent's voice snapped off as someone emerged from the gravity-chute and tapped her on the shoulder. "If it isn't Tarza Rhymer, up to her old tricks!" said Brig Meriwether pleasantly. "What a surprise!"

chapter 7

Team Song

Janna stared. "Coach! What are you doing here?"

"We're all here," said Meriwether. "Pav told me you had an audition so we all came to watch." He pointed up to the top of the statue where the other members of Gold Team Junior had popped into view. Pavros waved in a lordly manner.

"But –" Janna stared at the star-gypsy agent. "Do you know her?"

"I know of her. She preys on people who are young and talented, don't you, Rhymer? You promise them everything and then give them nothing."

"I've done nothing illegal," said Rhymer stiffly. "The Interstellar Star-Gypsy Contest is a registered trade name."

"Yes, but how many winners have actually become star-gypsies? None. I think you'd better be on your way before I call the lawpatrollers."

The agent glowered at him. "I'm not going anywhere until I get paid what I'm owed!"

"You're not owed anything," said Meriwether. "Under Station Law, children can't sign contracts without a parent or guardian. If I were you I'd think twice before trying to scam Stationers' children again." He looked severely at the twins. "And I

expect you two to do a lot more research before
you enter fake contests and agree to auditions."

Tarza Rhymer protested but, when Meriwether
put a call through to the lawpatrollers, she
hurriedly stepped into the gravity-chute and
then vanished from sight.

"Why did you let us go ahead with the audition
if it wasn't legal?" Janna asked plaintively.

Meriwether smiled at her. "I hoped you might
see through her for yourselves," he said. "If I'd
forbidden you as soon as Pav told me what was
happening, you would have blamed me for
spoiling your chances, right?"

Janna glanced at Jaff, who was staring at the ground.

"I wouldn't," she said.

"I would," admitted Jaff. He looked up at Coach Meriwether. "I suppose I should say thank you."

"You had already made your own decision," said Meriwether. He smiled. "I'm Shipborn too, Jaff, and I *know* how it feels to want to be someone special. And I think you will be touring in a few years. You and Janna did a lovely rendition of 'Ship Song'."

"Thanks," said Jaff, but he sounded gloomy. "So that wasn't a real contest at all?"

"It's real," said Meriwether. "But every single entry gets to the semi-finals. Every single entry gets an audition. Most of them back away, as you two did, but a few actually pay what she demands." He sighed. "Older people than you have been caught in this kind of scam. It's been going on for centuries."

Ellie clambered down from the viewing platform and tapped Meriwether on the arm. "Coach? We've had an idea... if you agree?"

"I never agree to anything until I know what it is," said Meriwether.

"We think it would be really good if we had a team song to sing before the game when we go to the finals. We could show everyone that 3D is not the *only* thing we're good at!"

"Sounds smart to me," said Meriwether. "But where would you find a good song, and who would teach you to sing it?"

"Well…" Ellie grinned at Jaff and Janna. "I don't think we'd have to look far."

"Neither do I," agreed Meriwether. "Now we have a practice… but, while Gold Team Junior throws balls about, maybe our official team musician will find us a winning song?"

Team Song
Nova Speak

3D A skilled ball game played on space stations.

Beeper A small communication device used on *Nova*.

Birth Mark An identity tattoo Stationborn have on their right forearm.

Blankout A newly invented material that renders things invisible.

Ear globe An earring shaped like planet Earth, worn by the Earthborn.

Earthborn People born on Earth.

Gravity-chute A cylinder in which gravity can be changed.

Green-ox system A system in which plants are grown to help provide oxygen.

Holoscreens Holographic screens, used for advertising.

Holoteam Holographic players, used to train 3D teams.

Lawpatrollers The police force on *Nova*.

Team Song
Nova Speak

Low-G Low gravity.

Nova A huge space station.

Shipborn People born on huge spaceships.

Spear-leap A move made by 3D players.

Star-gypsies Musicians who travel the galaxy, performing on starships, stations and planets.

Stationborn People born on big space stations, like *Nova*.

Up-and-over A move made by 3D players.